Morag Douglas
Margaret Iwa - Fiona McLeod

To Ava.

SCGOLI

Scgoli

Morag Douglas
Margaret I. Iwa
Fiona McLeod.

ISBN: 978-1-911424-21-5
SKU: 9781911424215

Cover and Layout: Wolf
Photo re-elaborated version: Wolf
Editor: Monica Turoni

Publishing company
Black Wolf Edition & Publishing Ltd.
1 Begg Road, Kirkcaldy KY2 6HD, Scotland
www.blackwolfedition.com

PREFACE

In a wee pub in Burntisland, on the Fife coast of Scotland, there is a small group of knitters who meet every Thursday night and sit in the corner knitting and chatting.

As the evening progresses, there is more chatting than knitting and on one occasion the subject turned to childhood toys that you no longer see. The night wore on, the conversation took a turn of its own and somehow or other they agreed to knit an updated Scottish version of an old favourite.

A pattern was written, wool was bought and Scgoli was born. Pretty soon he had his own Facebook page and was travelling all over the world. The knitters and their friends have had lots of fun with him and hope that when you get to know him, you will too.

(The Authors)

Chapter One

Hi, I am a Scgoli. For hundreds of years our clan has lived in burrows underneath the Binn which is a really big hill just behind the Fife seaside town of Burntisland in Scotland. We have always been quite content with our way of life and not really worried about what might be going on outside. We have of course seen signs of big people but all Scgolis are taught from an early age to keep well out of their way in case they get eaten or worse. I have never understood what could be worse than being eaten!

Because of that we don't really go out much as it's quite hard to hide when you have bright orange hair. Scgolis only venture out at night to look for food and anything else that might be useful.

Now that you know what he is, let me tell you a bit about who he is. He has never really been like the other

Scgolis because he has always been curious. Although life in the burrow is good and happy, he has always thought there must be more. Since he was a tiny Scgoli, he has peered out of the burrow at that enormous Scgoli coloured sky and thought that there must be more under it than just them and big people looking for Scgolis to eat. Although he had often wondered about it, he was still quite content with his life until one day last summer.

Summer is not good for Scgolis because even though there is more food, there is not so much dark and they have to spend more time squashed up together in their sweaty burrow. That day he was sitting just inside the door staring out at the big sky when he heard the most wonderful music.

He has found out that it was bagpipes and there was a big competition on in Burntisland. That day it made him feel all tingly inside and he decided that if there was music like that under the big sky, he was going to go out and see what else there was. And that's how his big adventure started.

Chapter Two

Once he had decided to leave that was it. No one was able to stop him whatever they said. He was even summoned to a meeting of the clan elders who tried their best to convince him that he was destined to be eaten within a day if he left. There was much tugging of beards and scratching of heads and eventually they shook their heads and said goodbye with a look in their eyes that said they were pretty sure they would never see him again. In his burrow his mum was crying, his dad wouldn't talk to anyone and his brothers and sisters were trying to look sad but he knew they were secretly looking forward to the extra space in the bed. He didn't like to tell them but his mum had a funny looking bump in her tummy that meant that there wouldn't be much extra space for long. The only person who seemed to understand was his old granny.

"Well laddie," she said, "you'll never know unless you go and see for yourself, and if you get eaten you'll know they were right."

Scgoli was pretty sure she hadn't thought that one through properly but he did appreciate the thought. Granny told him though that she had the same thoughts when she was a little Scolette but life, grandpa and kids got in the way and she never got the chance. Now she is old, bent over and walks with a stick, but someday Scgoli would come back and take his granny out to see whatever it is she missed. He really hopes there is something good out there.

On the day of his leaving they were all there to see him off apart from his dad who still wasn't talking. His granny handed him a parcel which contained a strange looking garment that she had knitted for him.

"Right my laddie, these are called pants," she explained, "I don't know much about big people but the old ones used to talk about them wearing things like these for some reason so I thought you should have some. I'm not really sure what they are for but you don't know what you are going to come up against out there so I think you should keep them on at all times. If nothing else they will keep you warm where it matters."

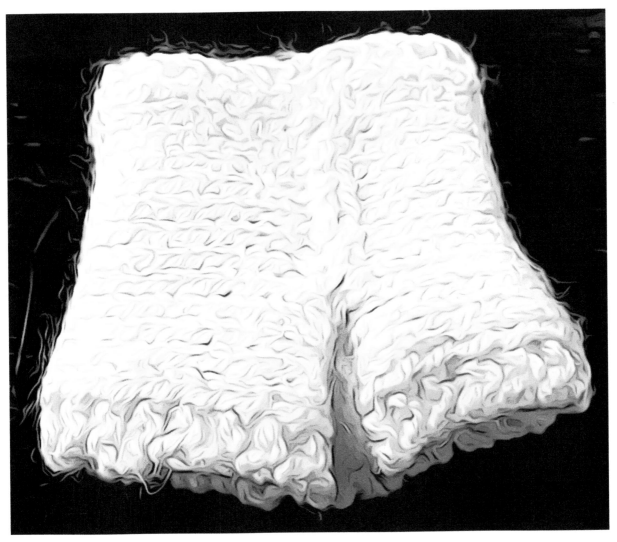

She made him put them on before he left and he had to promise that he would always keep them on whatever happened. They did feel awfully strange as Scgolis don't wear anything under the kilt but he had to admit they were quite cosy if a little prickly.

After another round of tearful hugs and kisses he was ready to go. Trying to look a lot braver than he felt, he crawled out of the burrow and set off down the hill with what he hoped looked like a purposeful stride.

The first thing he noticed was that everything was really big and he was really small. He tried to keep to the edge of the path to give him some cover but it was really overgrown and he was finding it hard going. He was making some progress and although it was slow, he knew he was going to make it down to the bottom eventually. There was no way he was going to turn back this early. After a while, he started to relax and look around. Things were so different in daylight and all the bright colours were amazing, in fact it was really quite pleasant being out during the day.

He was just starting to feel a bit more confident and even enjoying it when the earth began to shake under his feet. The shaking was getting stronger and stronger and he could hear something big coming really fast up the path towards him. In a moment of panic he scrambled up the nearest tree and clung on for dear life.

It was not a moment too soon as he had just made it to safety when two big horse monsters carrying big people thundered past him. If he had stayed down on the path he would surely have been trampled and the only good thing about that is that there would not have been much left of him to eat.

After they had passed he waited a little while until he had stopped shaking. Then he had a good look round to see if it was safe to climb down and carry on. The only problem was that he couldn't. Somehow he seemed to have got stuck in the tree and whichever way he moved or wriggled he couldn't get free.

At first he panicked but after a while he calmed down and tried to understand how he got stuck. It seemed that

granny Scgoli's knitted pants had got caught somewhere and he couldn't reach round to free them.

This was definitely going to be a problem. Granny had told him never to take the pants off, but he couldn't see how else he was going to get free. So he was faced with either taking the pants off — which would surely end in disaster — or staying up the tree for ever which wasn't such a great idea either.

"What am I to do?" he thought.

Chapter Three

Just then he heard the sound of some big people coming down the hill. He peered out from the tree and he could see them coming towards him. Although they looked big they didn't look too scary or hungry (which was a good thing), and their voices sounded quite gentle.

"Perhaps they might help me and then I could get out of the tree without having to take the pants off," thought Scgoli. "After all I was going to have to meet some big people sooner or later if I wanted to see everything under the big blue sky."

As they got closer, he took a deep breath and in his loudest voice he shouted, "Help please!"

Granny Scgoli always taught him that it doesn't cost anything to be polite and even though he didn't know if big people had manners or not, he thought it was best to be on the safe side. The big people stopped walking and one of them said, "Did you hear that?" The others shook their heads but they all had a bit of a look around anyway although none of them were looking up at the tree branch where he was stuck. They looked like they were going to walk on again so he summoned everything he had and roared: "HEEELP PLEEEASE!"

This time they all stopped and looked in his direction and finally one of them spotted his orange hair.

"Look! There is something orange in that tree. It almost looks like a tiny person with orange hair but it can't be, can it? I'm going for a closer look."

They all came over and peered up at him and when they were close enough he shouted down to them and explained his predicament. There was a bit of discussion but it sounded like they were all in agreement that he should be rescued and they were just deciding how best to do it.

The smallest of the three, who he assumed was

a younger big person, came forward and with the other two supporting her, she climbed up the tree until she could reach round behind him and free his pants.

She then very gently picked him out of the tree and passed him down to one of the other big people who carried him over to a fallen tree trunk and gently sat him down. The three big people then sat down beside him and looked at him.

"I have to admit that the thought of being eaten was in my mind at this point but I didn't want to appear ungrateful as they had just rescued me."

One of them took out a long tube thing from a bag she was carrying and unscrewed the lid then poured some sort of liquid into it. "Was this a sauce to dip me in?" Scgoli really hoped not.

Then to his surprise she held the lid in front of him and tipped it towards him.

"Have a little sip of tea," she smiled, "it will help with the shock and then maybe you could tell us who you are and how you got here."

That was a relief. He took a drink which was lovely and soon he began to feel a bit more like himself.

Sitting on the log sipping his tea he told the story of Scgolis, his decision to leave and find out what else was under the big sky and, of course, how he had come to be trapped in a tree by his pants.

The big people introduced themselves and they said they were very pleased to meet him and that his story

was extraordinary. They also reassured him that they had never met or heard of a Scgoli before and they had definitely never heard of anyone eating one. They were particularly impressed with his knitted pants and how he had taken such care of them as two of them were knitters themselves and were part of a knitting group. They said that the rest of the knitting group would love to meet him. If he liked, he could go home with one of them, they would introduce him to the rest of their group and then see if they could help him see as much as possible of what was under the big sky.

He thought that sounded amazing and that big people were every bit as nice as Scgolis were and maybe nicer in some cases (thinking of some Scgolis he knows). He was happy to go with them and meet their friends.

One of the big people tucked him into the top of the bag on her back so that he could see out and they set off down the hill towards his big adventure.

CREDITS

Burntisland and District Pipe Band (Pg. 9)

Photo re-elaborated version by Wolf

Hallon

Denairn Hill

Craigkelly

Rochanbraes

Crofsgates

Leehytenut

Denairn

Binend

Silly Barton

Bin Hill

head

BRUN TISLAND

Charter

Porthead

Grange

head

S.t Charter's Elq.

Jufkin Runs

Hobinton

Newbigging

Campbell Elq.

Catle

Kirktown

Lime Kilns

Claymr

Harb.

BRUNTISLAND

Commons

7

8

Hatton

Denairn Hill

Crosegates

Craigkelly

Roddinbra

Denairn

Lochylenat

Binend

Silly Barton

estlehead

Bin Hill

Craier

BRUN TISLAND

Woodhead

Grange

nhead

L. Hobinson

S. Charters Esq

Kirkin Ruins

Newbiding

P

Kirktown

Hill

Hird Campbell
Esq

Cattle

Harb.

Lime Ki
Clavn

BRUNTISLAND

Commons

7

← 8